First published in 2018 in Great Britain by
Barrington Stoke Ltd
18 Walker Street, Edinburgh, EH3 7LP

www.barringtonstoke.co.uk

Text © 2018 Philip Ardagh
Illustrations © 2018 Tom Morgan-Jones

A CIP catalogue record for this book is available
from the British Library upon request

ISBN: 978-1-78112-762-9

Printed in China by Leo

This book is in a super readable format for young readers
beginning their independent reading journey.

# Philip Ardagh

# Norman the Norman and the Very Small Duchess

Illustrated by
Tom Morgan-Jones

Barrington Stoke

*For all librarians everywhere,
however big or small.*

# Contents

# Chapter 1

# The Future Past

Norman the Norman from Normandy woke up with a big yawn and rolled over.

He kept rolling over and over and over and over.  You get the picture.

And if you don't get the picture, here's a picture.

See? A LOT of rolling over. And eyes wide open in surprise.

The reason WHY Norman the Norman from Normandy was so surprised was because when he normally rolled out of bed, he normally hit his bedroom floor with a THUMP.  And that was an end to it.  So, this time around – and around and around – he didn't know why he was STILL rolling.  And rolling.

Then he remembered. He hadn't gone to sleep in his bed the night before. He'd gone to sleep at the top of the hill.

If you're thinking 'WHY didn't he go to sleep in his bed?', that's a very good question. Which is why I am going to answer it.

## Chapter 2

# Conquest!

Meet William, Duke of Normandy. He was in charge of Normandy. Normandy was his dukedom, which is why he was called a duke. Or maybe Normandy was called his dukedom BECAUSE he was a duke. Either way, William, Duke of Normandy, was very proud of his Norman nose.

One day, the Duke was sitting in his castle when his wife came into the room. She was small. Very small. She was the kind of person who was so small that even small people called her small.

Even mice pointed and laughed at her. Look. Here's one and that's EXACTLY what it's doing.

"Hello, Mat," the Duke said. His wife's name was Matilda, but he called her "Mat" for short because everything ABOUT her was short.

"Hello," Matilda said. "Have you heard about Norman?"

"Is that the boy who saved a cart full of nuns from sinking in a stinking swamp, then saved the swamp from developers, then saved the developers from an angry dragon by telling the dragon that dragons don't exist?"

"Yes, that's the one," Matilda said with a nod.

"Then yes," said the Duke. "I have heard of him."

And yes, dear reader, that's the same Norman the Norman who goes rolling down that hill. Only it HASN'T HAPPENED YET. We've gone back to BEFORE the hill-rolling happened to find out how it came to pass.

"I think he should come on your conquest thingy with you," said Matilda.

In truth, William, Duke of Normandy, got cross when his wife called his

plans for the Conquest of England
his "conquest thingy". He wanted his
conquest to be big and brave and grand
and CONQUESTY.

"Conquest thingy" made it sound like
something you might stop off to do on
the way to the shops, if you remember
and have the time. William's plan was
to sail over to England, conquer it and
become KING.

But William did like Matilda's idea of asking Norman along.

"I need the very best Normans at my side when we conquer England, and there are many tales told about young Norman and his bravery," he said. "I'll order him to come to my castle right now."

## Chapter 3

## Captured!

There was a knock at Norman the Norman from Normandy's front door. It was Barry, the Duke's messenger. Barry was a bit nervous about knocking. He had heard stories about the tiny young Norman who didn't know the meaning of the word "fear".

Tales of Norman's bravery – and tales of how he didn't know the meaning of some words – were told around the fire.  And if people were too poor to afford firewood or, at the very least, a box of matches, then they would tell tales around their PRETEND fire, or where their fire would be if they had one.

Barry, the Duke's messenger, knocked again.  Harder this time.

Norman was busy trying to put up a picture.  The first thing was to hammer a nail into the wall with the hilt – handle – of his sword.

No.  That's not true.

The first thing Norman had to do was to stand on Truffle's back, to reach the spot where he had to hammer in the nail.  Truffle was Norman's not-so-wild

boar. Norman rode him instead of a
horse. And he used him instead of a
ladder for small jobs around the house.
Norman was up on Truffle's back when
Barry did the second, louder, knock.

Truffle was in a daydream about
acorns. He jumped in surprise and
charged. He banged through the front
door, without opening it, as Norman held
on tight.

Barry was startled.  He threw himself to the side to be safe.  He fell to the dusty ground with a THUNK!  A shower of great big splinters of front door fell down on top of him.

"Sorry!" Norman shouted, at the very moment that Truffle decided to stop in his tracks.  But Norman kept on going. He flew through the air and landed in a bush.

"Ooof!"

There was a cry of pain, and it wasn't
from Norman.  Norman looked down
and saw that he'd landed on someone.
What he didn't know was that this was a
robber.  The robber had been following
Barry, the Duke's messenger, for the last
three miles.  The robber rolled out into
the open with Norman on top of him.
Norman still had his sword in his hand.

"I s-surrender!" the robber said.

"Oh," Norman said. "Good ... I think."

Barry the messenger was stunned. Norman must have spotted the robber and grabbed his sword off him before the front door had even opened! All the stories about Norman the Norman from Normandy were true!

"Here," the robber said as he sat up. "Are you Great Big Norman's boy, Norman?"

Norman nodded. His helmet tilted forward and covered his eyes. "I am," he said.

"Then it's a great honour to be captured by you," the robber said. "Have a croissant." He reached inside his tunic, pulled out a croissant and handed it to Norman, who was still sitting on him. It was only a bit squashed (a bit like the robber himself).

"Thank you," Norman said.

"It's still fresh," the robber said. "I stole it this morning."

Barry was up on his feet again. He dusted himself down. "I'm sorry to bother you," he said as he walked over to the mighty Norman. All of a sudden, he was worried that Norman might not WANT to come to the Duke's castle. And what could he do then?  "William, your Duke, told me to ask you to come to his castle at once," he told Norman.

Norman climbed off the robber. "Really?" he said.  "I like castles.  Does it have a moat?"

"Well, it has a ditch all the way round it," said Barry.  "A very deep ditch."

"But that's not quite the same as a moat, is it?" Norman said. "What about a gift shop?"

Barry thought hard. "Well, the Duke does sometimes give people nice presents."

Norman still wasn't sure. "Does it have a tea room?" he asked.

Barry thought of the Duke of Normandy's enormous banqueting hall. Perfect for enormous banquets. "Yes," he said. "A really good one."

"My mum and I do like a castle with a good tea room," Norman said. "I'll come."

## Chapter 4

# What a Welcome!

Norman the Norman rode into the courtyard of the Duke's castle. There was Duchess Matilda, ready to greet him. The first thing he saw was that she was a sensible size. She was about the same size as him.

On the way to William's castle, he and Barry had stopped so that Truffle could have a drink of water. But then Norman had tripped over the end of his belt, which was hanging down, and he'd fallen forward.

Somehow his Norman broadsword ended up stuck in the chest of Normandy's last remaining giant.

The giant had been hiding between two very big trees at the side of the road.  (He was pretending to be a third very big tree.)  The last remaining giant – who was no longer remaining – fell to the ground as lifeless as a very big sack of dead rocks.

"Blimey!" Barry said, which is Norman for "God blind me!"  (Or, if it isn't, it should be.)

A crowd of people from the village came to see the dead giant and cheered. He'd been bothering them for months – he'd stolen their food, sat on their houses and drunk all the water from their ponds.

One family took the shirt off the giant's body and then made it into eleven pairs of curtains, a sail for a boat, a tent, some dish cloths and – er – a much smaller shirt. But this didn't all happen at once. They were still busy trying to pull the shirt off the dead giant as Norman the Norman and Barry left.

The first thing the Duchess Matilda spotted when she first laid eyes on Norman was that Norman was every bit as small as she hoped he would be. She marched across the cobbles of the castle courtyard and looked him in the eye. She didn't even have to climb on a pile of egg boxes to do it.

Their eyes were the same distance from the ground.  Matilda gave an excited squeal and did an excited little jump up into the air.  (She could only do little jumps.)

The jump gave her lady-in-waiting, Lady Marie, a bit of a shock.  It was Lady Marie's job to follow Matilda around everywhere and to wait – she was the lady-in-waiting, after all.

Lady Marie wasn't sure what she was waiting for. So she kept on waiting, to find out.

"Welcome!" Matilda said, and she threw her arms wide.

Norman the Norman wasn't sure what the correct way to greet the Duchess was, so he copied what she did – he threw HIS arms wide too.

Yes, of course he was holding his dad's great big heavy sword. The sword cut the bottom of a wooden dovecote in half. The dovecote fell to the ground – and it only just missed Norman's friend and pet toad, Toad – and then startled white doves came flapping out.

The doves all perched on the nearest thing, which was Norman the Norman from Normandy with his arms out wide. He looked like a cross made of white doves.

If there isn't a picture of this here, there should be.

Thank you.  And what a splendid picture it is too.

Matilda had never seen anything like it.  It was like the best greeting EVER.

"It tickles," Norman said.

But, because his mouth was full of white feathers, no one could understand what he was saying.

## Chapter 5

## Nosh

A banquet had been prepared in Norman's honour. A pile of books was put on Norman's chair so that he could see over the top of the banqueting table. Back then, books were written by hand, bound in leather and cost a LOT of money. So it was very special for Norman to be allowed to park his bottom on top of them.  Normally, only the Duchess was allowed to sit on books.

Servants were busy putting pewter platters piled high with mouth-watering goodies on the table.  There were no knives and forks because no one had got around to inventing forks yet.  They didn't have the tine.*

*This is a fork joke which only works if –

a) you know that the right word for the prong of a fork is a *tine*, and

b) you think waste of *tine* sounds a bit like waste of *time*.

And they didn't put knives on the table because everyone used their own dagger.

William, Duke of Normandy, had just made a nice speech to welcome Norman and say how proud he was that Norman would be part of the Norman invasion going over to England to claim the English crown.

Of course, Norman was only half-listening. (He was feeding titbits to Truffle, who was lying next to his chair like a dog with big tusks.) Norman thought that the crown was just that – a crown that went on someone's head. He thought that claiming the crown would be like going into his local baker's shop and claiming a free croissant.

Norman didn't understand that William meant that he was going to fight to become KING OF ENGLAND.  And that Norman would be one of the soldiers to fight with him.

When they'd all sat down to eat the feast, Norman remembered that he didn't have a dagger of his own.  He looked around.

"Please," the man next to him said. He was Odo, Bishop of Bayeux (which rhymes with mayo, which is short for a sort of fancy salad cream). "Use one of my daggers. I always carry a spare." He leaned forward and pulled a dagger from his boot. He wiped it on his sleeve and handed it to Norman.

"No need, thank you," Norman said.
He took out his broadsword, but he
couldn't balance it.  The broadsword
swished across the table, towards the
Duke.

Everyone in eye-shot looked on in
HORROR.

## Chapter 6

## Ooops!

Once in a while, people tried to kill William. Not simply because he was William but because he was the Duke of Normandy and they wanted his job. It was the top job in Normandy. No one could tell you what to do.

Anyone who tried to kill William ended up:

- being given a stern telling-off

- tortured

- then executed.

It was lucky for the Duke AND for Norman that Norman's Norman broadsword missed William.

A servant was about to pour a drink from a large jug into William's goblet. The tip of the sword hit the jug instead.

The jug smashed into 22 bits. Drink went everywhere. Duke William jumped to his feet. He didn't want to get soaked, and he didn't like the look of THE BIG BROADSWORD.

Toad sat in the middle of the table.
He was soaking wet.  He gave a massive
burp for a toad (which was still a big
burp for a human).

BURP!

Matilda jumped to her feet. This made her look even smaller, because she was taller when she was sitting on HER pile of books on HER chair. She clapped her hands in delight. "Norman just saved your life, William!" she yelped.

'Have I?' Norman thought.

"How so?" the Duke asked.

"Didn't you see?" Matilda said. "That toad was in the jug. One of the most poisonous kinds of toad there is! So poisonous that it will have poisoned the

drink!  The very drink you were about to drink!"

William, Duke of Normandy, peered at Toad.  "Are you sure it's not a frog?"

"Ribbet," Toad said.  He used to spend a lot of time with frogs.

"See?" the Duke said.  "That's a frog! Frogs say 'Ribbet'!"

'Oh, there you are, Toad,' Norman thought. 'I didn't know where you'd hopped off to.'

Matilda pulled the top book off the stack of books on her chair. "Look!" she said, and pointed. The book was called MY FIRST BIG BOOK OF TOADS.

The tiny duchess used both hands to open the huge leather book.

Inside, the book was beautiful.
Everything was written in hand in Latin
by someone who was very good with a
pen.  Some of the bigger letters had little
pictures drawn inside them in bright
colours, including gold.  And some of
the pages were taken up with one big
picture of one big toad.  The Duchess
Matilda flipped through the pages until
she came to one picture which looked a
LOT like Toad.

"There!" Matilda said, and she pointed in triumph.

Toad tilted his head to admire the picture this way, then that.  If he'd had a pen with him, I think he might have signed it with his name.

The Duke came around the table, bent down and threw his arms around Norman the Norman. "You saved my life!" he said. "Thank you!"

"My pleasure," Norman said. He didn't tell William that Toad was HIS toad. Why bother such an important man with such an unimportant detail?

Toad jumped up onto Norman's helmet.

"Ribbet," he said.  It was the only noise Toad ever made, apart from burps.

## Chapter 7

## All the Latest News

A very small, very old lady scuttled out from under the banqueting table and started to sew very fast indeed.

She looked up at Norman. "How do?" she said, and rubbed her nose on her sleeve.

"H-Hello," Norman said. He turned to Bishop Odo and asked in a soft voice, "Who's she?"

"She's Gran," Odo said. "She works for me. As well as being Bishop of Bayeux, I run a local news-tapestry."

"What's a news-tapestry?" asked Norman.

"It's an embroidery that reports all the local news in pictures," the bishop explained.

"If it's an embroidery, why do you call it a news-tapestry and not a news-embroidery?" Norman asked.

"Because a news-tapestry sounds more high-tech," Bishop Odo explained. "Tapestries are made with LOOMS, and a loom is a machine. People love machines! It sounds much more exciting than a room full of old ladies doing embroidery with their needles."

"Oh," said Norman.

"Ribbet," said Toad on his helmet.

Odo looked at Toad nervously. "I think he likes you," he said.

"And I like him," said Norman.

"Good," Odo said, and he told Norman more about the news-tapestry. "I have people called news-recorders whose job it is to embroider all the latest news. Gran here is one of them. She's live at the scene, reporting on your arrival at the castle. Look."

He held up one end of the embroidery that the little old lady was working on. It was beautiful – a picture in embroidery of Norman smashing the jug. The Duke looked startled and Toad was jumping out.

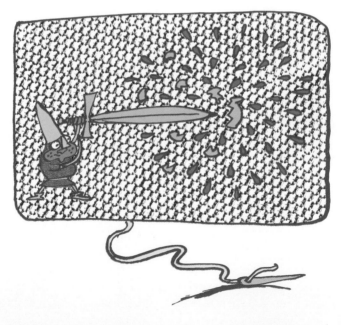

"Wow," Norman said. "That IS good. And she's your gran?"

"No, no, no," Odo said. "Gran is her name. I think it's short for Grandmother. I'm William's half-brother," he went on. "I'll fight with William when he conquers England, but because I'm a bishop, it would be wrong if I had a sword."

"I see." Norman nodded. Toad nodded too. He had to nod whether he liked it or not, because he was sitting on Norman's helmet.

"I can't have a sword," said Odo. "So I use a club. A really BIG club. Gran will come with us to England," he went on. "She will record our victory over the English."

"Victory? Are we going to win, then?" Norman asked as he bit into something that had been put in front of him. It was a pewter plate and it hurt his teeth.

Bishop Odo gave him a look. "Well, we're not going all the way over there to lose, are we?"

"Great," said Norman.

## Chapter 8

# The Selfie Embroidery

After the banquet, the Duchess Matilda
stood next to Norman in front of the
best mirror in the palace. They looked
at themselves in the mirror, and
Duchess Matilda did a quick embroidery
that showed her and Norman standing
side by side.

"What are you doing, lady duke person?" Norman asked. He tried to sound as polite as possible.

"It's called a selfie," Matilda told him. "You are a great ambassador for little people, Norman. You show that heroes come in ALL shapes and sizes."

Toad jumped back up onto Norman's helmet. (He had been too shy to be in the selfie embroidery.)

"No more chit-chat!" Duke William said with a smile. He walked across the stone floor and gave Norman a friendly slap on the back.

The slap on the back was so hard it made Norman lurch forward. He missed the mirror and bumped into a tapestry hanging on the wall. There was a spy hiding behind it, who now toppled out of a window with a cry.

This cry, in fact:

"Arrrrrrrrrrrrrrrrrrrrrrrrrrrrrrrrr rrrrrrrrrrrrrrrrrgh!"

The spy would have landed in the moat with a loud SPLASH if there had been a moat.  As it was, he landed in the ditch with a less cheery CRUNCH.

A group of soldiers peered out of the window at the same time as another lot ran downstairs to find out who the spy was and what he'd been up to.

"You're a one-man army!" the Duke said. He turned back to Norman and gave him a hug. "You keep saving my life! Tomorrow, we sail for England and I want you by my side."

## Chapter 9

## On a Roll

And so the Duke and his army made their way to the seaside, where the ships waited for them on the beach.

"Tomorrow the conquest begins!" he said. "Tonight we set up camp!"

William was a duke, so he didn't have to do any setting up of the camp himself. He had a whole ARMY to do that for him. While that was going on, Norman and Truffle went for a walk. Truffle found a rather fine stash of acorns, so by the time they got back, most of the others had gone to bed. And Norman didn't know which was HIS tent, so Norman and Truffle decided to sleep side by side under the stars.

In the night, Norman rolled over in his sleep and kept on rolling. He opened his eyes in surprise. Yes, it was THAT rolling over. The one at the beginning of this story. When Norman got to the bottom, the rolling stopped and he sat up. Toad hopped back up onto his helmet. Truffle bounded down the hill after them. This was out of loyalty and love, and also because he knew Norman had some of those fine acorns left in his pocket.

"Well," said Norman as he got up onto the not-so-wild boar, "we may as well go home now."

He arrived at his house just as his mother, Norma the Norman from Normandy, was out front.

Norma was a very strong woman. Her job was to bend bent iron bars straight. She was getting ready for her day when she saw Norman. "Hello, son,"

she said as she gave Norman a hug.
"Where have you been?"

"I went to look around a castle,"
Norman said.

"Did it have a moat?" she asked.

Norman shook his head.  "No, but it
did have a big ditch all the way round."

"That's not quite the same," Norma
said.  "What about a gift shop?"

Norman shook his head again. "No.
But it had a nice tea room. More of a
banqueting hall, I suppose."

"Lovely," Norma said. "You're just in
time for breakfast. Your egg should be
ready."

"Thanks, Mum," said Norman, and he walked into his house and straight to the kitchen with a slight limp.  (The limp was because of that mother/son hug he'd just had.)

Norman lifted his Norman broadsword, ready to cut the top off his egg.

Norma smiled at the loud CRASHES and BANGS, and at the cry of their servant as he ducked for cover.

It was good to have Norman home.

# An Afterword

Bishop Odo went on to produce a special edition of the Bayeux Tapestry – which was really an embroidery. It was all about William's victory in England (where he became king). Matilda became England's smallest ever queen (so far). Bishop Odo used English embroiderers to sew the so-called tapestry because they were cheaper. And, of course, Norman, Truffle and Toad aren't in the Bayeux Tapestry because they missed the boat. But Odo is. With his great big bishop's club.